Ralegan Siddhi: A Special Community

Carmel Reilly

NELSON CENGAGE Learning™

Australia • Brazil • Japan • Korea • Mexico • Singapore • Spain • United Kingdom • United States

Ralegan Siddhi: A Special Community

Fast Forward
Gold Level 22

Text: Carmel Reilly
Editor: Cameron Macintosh
Design: Vonda Pestana
Series design: James Lowe
Production controller: Seona Galbally
Photo research: Gillian Cardinal
Audio recordings: Juliet Hill, Picture Start
Spoken by: Matthew King and Abbe Holmes
Reprint: Jennifer Foo

Acknowledgements
The author and publisher would like to acknowledge permission to reproduce material from the following sources:
Front and back covers: Dinodia Photo Library
AAP Image/AP Photo/Gurinder Osan, pp 9/ AAP Image/AP Photo/Ajay Kumar Singh, p 15 bottom; Photolibrary/ Roger Hutchings/Alamy, p 5; Corbis, p 15 top; Dinodia Photo Library, pp 3-4, 6-8,10-14, 16-23.

ISBN 978 0 17 012690 8
ISBN 978 0 17 012681 6 (set)

Cengage Learning Australia
Level 7, 80 Dorcas Street
South Melbourne, Victoria Australia 3205
Phone: 1300 790 853

Cengage Learning New Zealand
Unit 4B Rosedale Office Park
331 Rosedale Road, Albany, North Shore NZ 0632
Phone: 0508 635 766

For learning solutions, visit cengage.com.au

Printed in Australia by Ligare Pty Ltd
4 5 6 7 8 9 10 21 20 19 18 17

Evaluated in independent research by staff from the Department of Language, Literacy and Arts Education at the University of Melbourne.

Ralegan Siddhi: A Special Community

Carmel Reilly

Contents

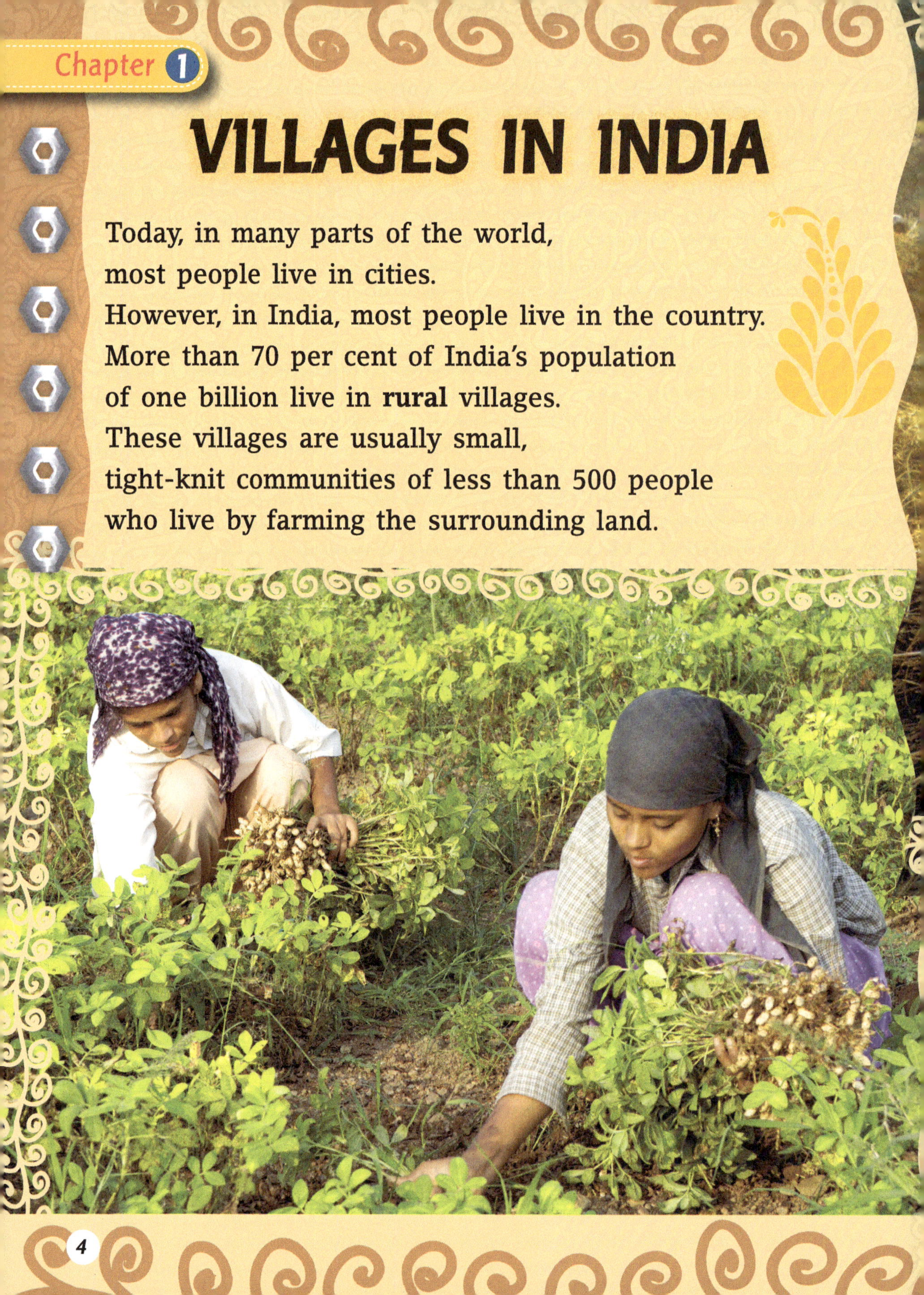

Chapter 1

VILLAGES IN INDIA

Today, in many parts of the world, most people live in cities. However, in India, most people live in the country. More than 70 per cent of India's population of one billion live in **rural** villages. These villages are usually small, tight-knit communities of less than 500 people who live by farming the surrounding land.

Life in many of these villages is hard.
People rely on farming to get by,
and if there is drought or the crops fail,
there is no other kind of employment to fall back on.
Increasingly, men from villages move to cities
to find work so they can send money back
to their families.

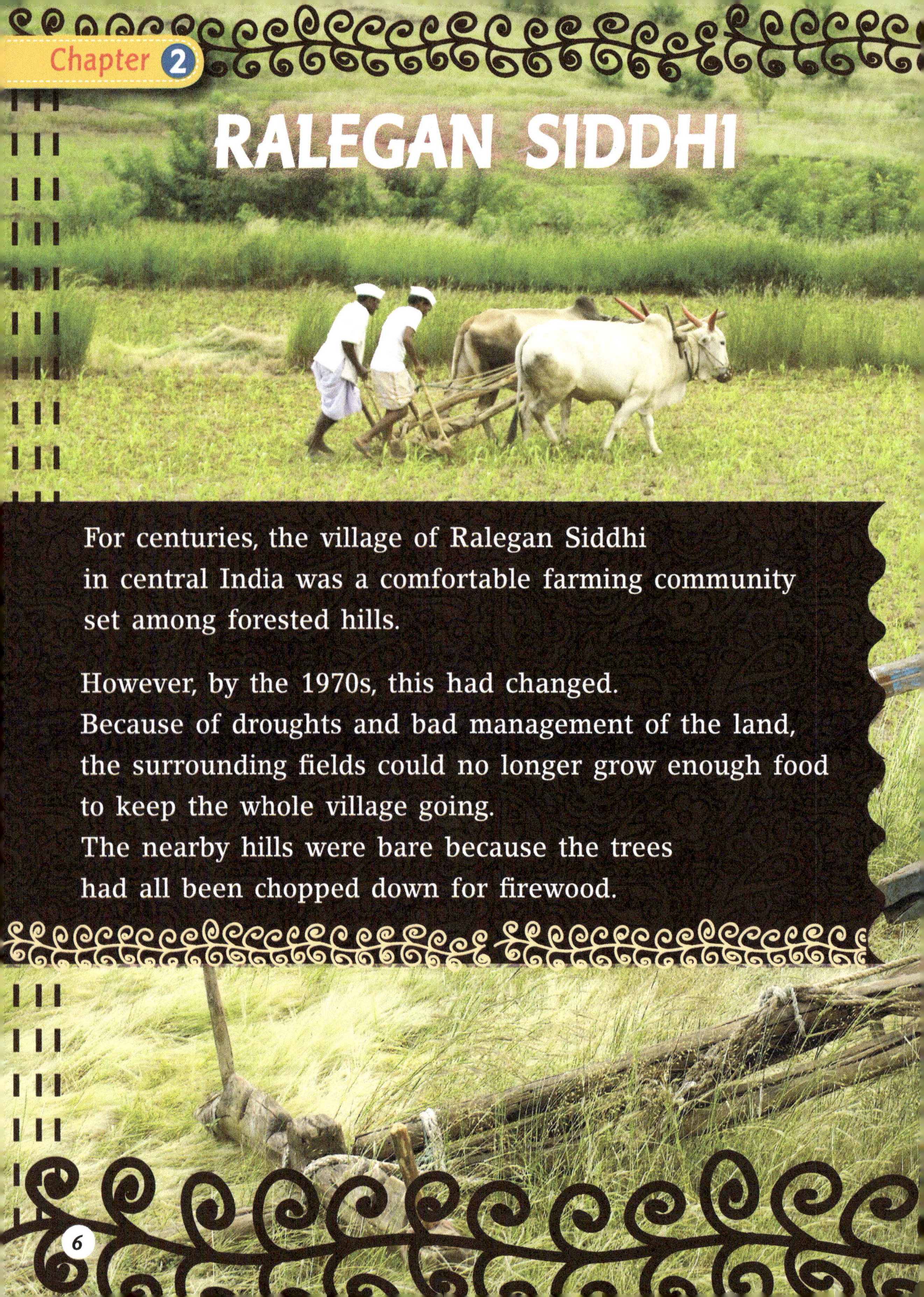

Chapter 2

RALEGAN SIDDHI

For centuries, the village of Ralegan Siddhi in central India was a comfortable farming community set among forested hills.

However, by the 1970s, this had changed. Because of droughts and bad management of the land, the surrounding fields could no longer grow enough food to keep the whole village going. The nearby hills were bare because the trees had all been chopped down for firewood.

The only way for many families to survive was to make illegal alcohol.
This in turn led to lawlessness and drunkenness and the breakdown of village life.

Running Words 201

Ralegan Siddhi today

Chapter 3

ANNA HAZARE, A MAN WITH A VISION

Anna Hazare was born in India in 1940.
In the 1950s, his family moved to Ralegan Siddhi.
The family was poor, so Anna moved to Mumbai,
one of India's largest cities, to find work.
In his twenties, he joined the Indian army,
but whenever he had **leave**,
he went back to visit his family in the village.

Anna Hazare in recent years

In 1975, Anna left the army
and returned to Ralegan Siddhi for good.
Although the place had grown poor
and lawless over the years,
Anna went back with a vision of improving it.

The first thing Anna did was to give up all his savings to start the **renovation** of the village temple, which was beginning to fall down.

village temple

Next, he vowed to stay unmarried and to give up all his money, land and worldly goods so that he could put his energy into the village.

Anna could see that there were two areas of village life that needed a lot of improvement –
one was environmental and the other was social.
He saw that people's lives would not get better unless the environment was improved.
But he knew that the environment would not change until people learned to work together.

Chapter 4

THE SOCIETY

Although he had ideas about how to make Ralegan Siddhi a better place, Anna wanted the people of the village to get together and decide for themselves what they wanted.

The first thing that people said they wanted
was an end to lawlessness.
This meant no more alcohol.
Everyone from the village took a vow at the temple
to stop making and drinking alcohol.

Having an Equal Say

Most Indian villages have a council, usually made up of men from the top caste. However, in Ralegan Siddhi, the people agreed that a range of groups should have an equal say in decision-making.

A council was then formed that included people from all castes.

The Caste System

Indian society is divided up into many groups called 'castes'.
Castes are ranked from high to low,
and those in the high castes have more power and wealth than those in lower castes.

a man of high caste

There are millions of people in India called Dalits.
This group was once called the Untouchables,
and they are seen as the lowest caste in society.

Dalits

Taking Care of Everyone

The people of Ralegan Siddhi came to realise that they could not move forward as a group unless the weakest members were taken care of first.

The village was given loans by the government to help the Dalits buy land and animals.

The people from the higher castes in the village also made sure that the Dalits were included in social events, to help break down social barriers.

THE ENVIRONMENT

One of the reasons that Ralegan Siddhi had become so poor by the 1970s was because of soil erosion and lack of water. Anna Hazare talked the local government into providing money for rain water tanks so water could be collected. Money was borrowed to drill for wells near the village so that people did not have to walk so far to get water.

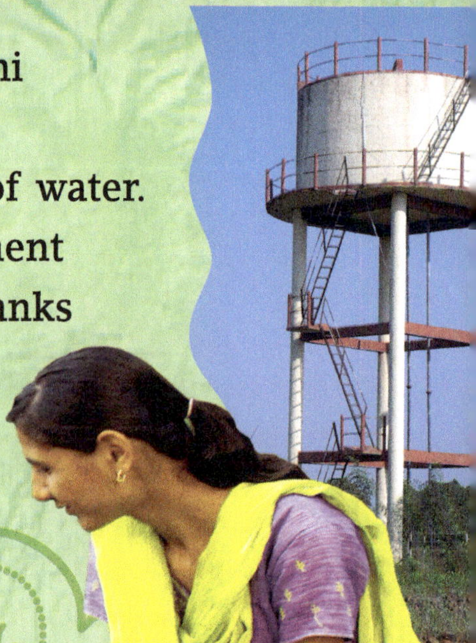

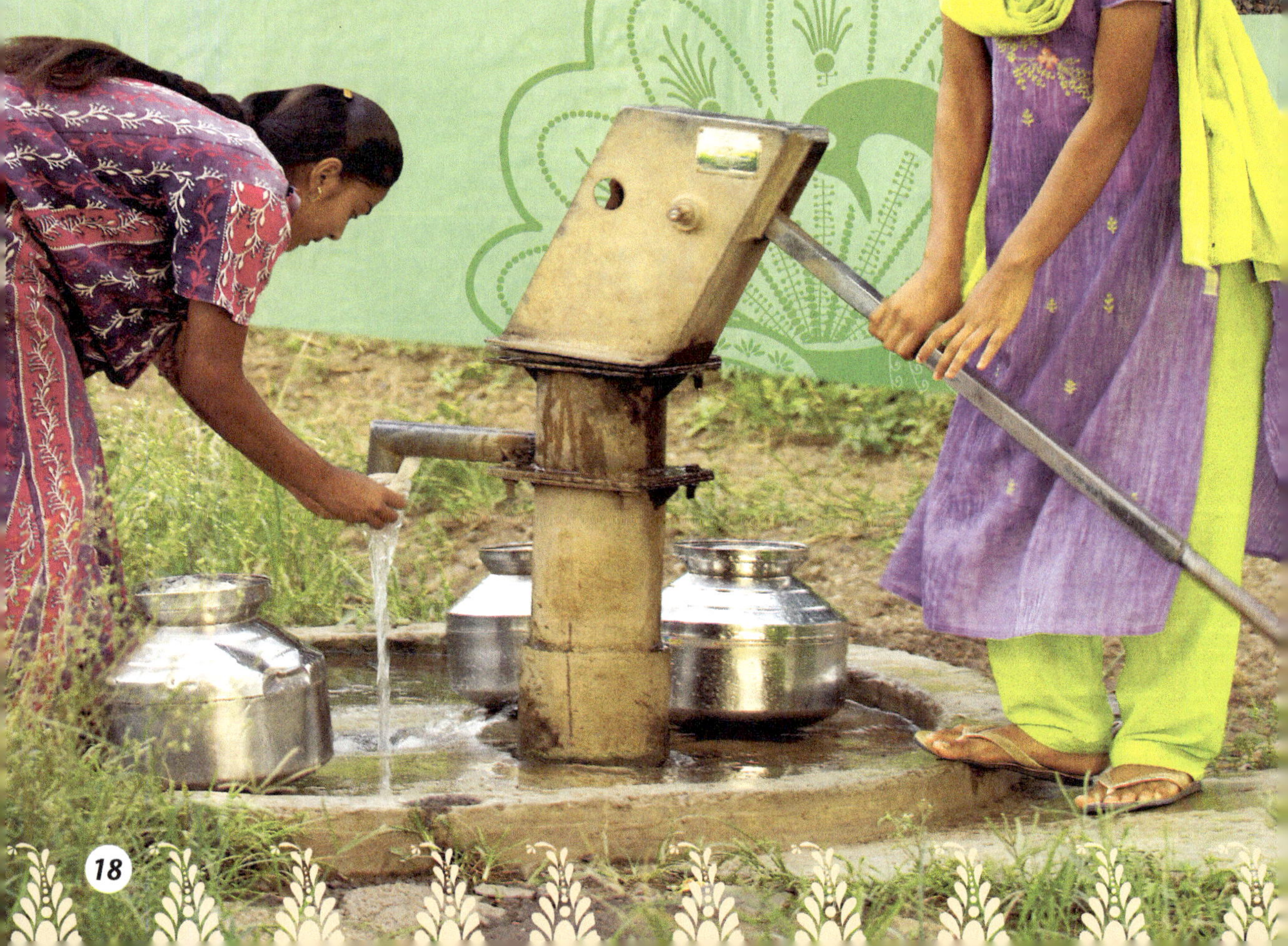

When there was more water available,
a program of tree planting began, to help stop erosion
and provide shade and firewood.

Milk and Grain

With more land available,
people were able to keep milking cows.

The cows were able to produce more milk
than the village needed, and the extra milk was sold.

Better land and more water also led to bigger grain crops.

Whenever there was extra grain,
it was put into the village **grain bank**
and stored for whoever might need it in the future.

Chapter 6

RALEGAN SIDDHI TODAY

Today, Ralegan Siddhi is not a wealthy place, but the people who live there have a good lifestyle and a lot to look forward to.

Most of the children of the village now go to primary school, and a new high school is being built.

People come from all around the country – and the world – to see how Ralegan Siddhi works. It is used as an example for many other poor communities of how change is possible.

Glossary

grain bank a place where grain is stored for future use

leave time taken away from a person's job

renovation restoring something to its original condition

rural in the countryside

Index